RACE
AGAINST TIME

Adaptation from the animated series: Anne Paradis
Illustrations: ROI VISUAL

CRACKBOOM!

Helly watches his friends racing on the track. He can't race with them because he's a helicopter.

Helly feels sad. He would like to drive, too.

Helly asks Jin to put wheels on him,
but Jin says no.
"Aw, please, Jin! Please!" Helly insists.
"All I want to do is race on the track. I'm
always on my own up there in the sky."
"I'm not putting wheels on you," says Jin.
"You're not a car, you're a helicopter."
Helly is very disappointed.

After practice, Jin tells Poli, Roy and Amber that Helly would like to have wheels too, so he could race with them.
"I didn't know Helly was feeling left out," Poli says sadly.

"Don't worry, he'll probably just change his mind," Jin replies.

Meanwhile, down at the Broomstown harbor, Helly has finished checking the electrical panel.
Helly still feels sad. He tells Camp he would like to drive like a car.

"If you really want to have wheels, here you go!"
Camp says. Helly feels so lucky.

"I'll trade the wheels for your propeller!" Camp says mischievously.

Helly hesitates. Jin would be really angry with him. But he wants the wheels very much.
"Sure!" he says to Camp. "The propeller is yours."

Helly races past Miss Belle and Lifty without his propeller.
"Look out, I'm coming through!" Helly laughs.
"A helicopter on wheels. Now we've seen it all!" says Miss Belle.

When Helly returns to headquarters with his new equipment, the Robocar rescue team gets a big surprise.

"Where did you get those wheels? What happened to your propeller?" Jin asks. Helly ignores Jin's questions and zooms off to test his new wheels on the race track.

But Helly isn't used to driving on wheels. He goes around a corner too fast and crashes.

Yahoo!

Bang!

His friends hurry over to help. "I think I broke my tail wing," says Helly. He feels sorry for himself.

Jin is very angry.

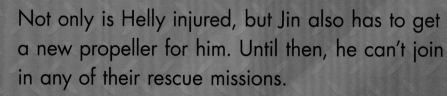

Not only is Helly injured, but Jin also has to get a new propeller for him. Until then, he can't join in any of their rescue missions.

When she's done fixing him up, Jin reminds Helly why wheels are dangerous for a helicopter.

"You're Helly the Helicopter, not Helly the Race Car. We're all different, so we can't all do the same things."
Helly feels misunderstood.

Meanwhile, Camp has fitted the propeller to his roof. He loves flying high in the sky.
"Look at me, I'm flying!" he cries.

Miss Belle and Lifty are worried he's going to have an accident. They tell him to come back down to the ground.

But Camp won't listen. He flies very high and tries to go faster. But he goes too fast, and suddenly the propeller breaks.

"Oh, no! Help!" Camp cries, as he falls from the sky and crash-lands on the roof of the warehouse.

Miss Belle calls Rescue Team
Headquarters for help.
She says Camp is in trouble.
It's an emergency, and they
have to hurry!

Poli, Roy and Amber
come to the rescue!

Down at the harbor,
Camp is in great danger.
He's about to fall through
the roof.
"Help me! I'm scared!"

Roy extends his crane
and Poli climbs onto the
roof to help Camp.

But the roof is too badly damaged. Poli can't get close to Camp. If he does, they might fall.

Poli hears a noise in the sky. It's Helly with his new propeller! Phew! Just in time! Helly connects Camp to the crane right as the roof caves in!

Roy holds Camp steady with the crane.
Then he winches him down to the
ground gently. Amber has a safety
cushion ready for a soft landing.

Luckily, Camp isn't badly hurt.
He only has a few scratches.

"I'm so glad our team is running at full power again," says Poli. "It wasn't the same without you, Helly. We really needed your help to rescue Camp."
Helly's happy to be flying again too.

The whole team gathers around outside the building.
"If Helly hadn't shown up when he did, you could've been badly hurt, Camp," Amber says.

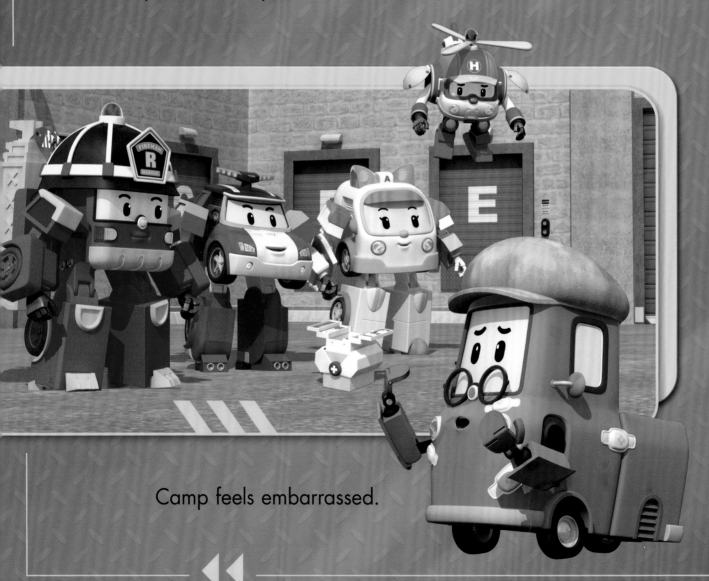

Camp feels embarrassed.

Helly apologizes.
"It's all my fault. I should never have traded my propeller for Camp's wheels. It was dangerous for us both. I'm sorry I caused so much trouble."

"And we're sorry that you were feeling so left out," says Roy. "You know, I wish I could fly like you."

"And sometimes I wish I had your strength, Roy," Poli adds.

"Sometimes I'd really like to drive as fast as you, Poli," says Amber.

Everyone laughs. "I guess we all wish we could be like each other sometimes," Helly says.

"We like you just the way you are, Helly," Amber replies. "Please don't change again!"

"Okay, I promise!" Helly says. "Now I know I'm made to fly. We're all different, and that's what makes us special."

Well said, Helly!

CrackBoom! Books is an imprint of Chouette Publishing (1987) Inc.

Text: adaptation by Anne Paradis of the animated series Robocar Poli, produced by ROI Visual.
All rights reserved.
Original script written by Ji Min AHN
Original episode #404: Helly's Wish

Illustrations:  © ROI VISUAL / EBS All rights reserved.

Chouette Publishing would like to thank the Government of Canada and SODEC
for their financial support.

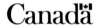

Canada

Québec ✚✚
Books Tax Credit   Gestion SODEC

Bibliothèque et Archives nationales du Québec and Library and Archives
Canada cataloguing in publication

Paradis, Anne 1972-,

[Course contre la montre. English]
Race against time/text, Anne Paradis; illustrations, Roi Visual; translation,
David Warriner.

(Robocar Poli)
(CrackBoom! Books)
Translation of: Course contre la montre.

Target audience: For children aged 3 and up.

ISBN 978-2-924786-88-8 (softcover)

I. Warriner, David, translator. II. Roi Visual (Firm), illustrator. III. Title.
IV. Title: Course contre la montre. English.

PS8631.A713C6813 2018   j843'.6   C2018-941655-6
PS9631.A713C6813 2018

Printed in Canada
10 9 8 7 6 5 4 3 2 1   CHO2043 AUG2018

MIX
Paper from
responsible sources
FSC® C103304